A Christmas

EVE TALE

Simon Mortimer

AuthorHouse™ UK
1663 Liberty Drive
Bloomington, IN 47403 USA
www.authorhouse.co.uk
UK TFN: 0800 0148641 (Toll Free inside the UK)
UK Local: 02036 956322 (+44 20 3695 6322 from outside the UK)

This book is printed on acid-free paper.

ISBN: 978-1-6655-8989-5 (sc)
ISBN: 978-1-6655-8990-1 (e)

Print information available on the last page.

Published by AuthorHouse 11/05/2021

authorHOUSE

A Christmas Eve Tale

It was Christmas eve; the longest day of all time!
Filled with anticipation, the air filled with Christmas rhyme.
All down the street and up our road,
The seeds of Christmas in children's heads had been sowed,
The houses were decorated from top to bottom,
And a treat for Santa, and his reindeer not forgotten.

Children were snuggled up warm in their beds,
While dreams of Christmas flickered in their heads.
The stockings and sacks were hung out with care,
In hopes that Santa Claus soon would be there.

Mum and I were all wrapped up in bed,
Looking forward to the magic of the day ahead.
When out on the front I heard a faint jingle jangle,
I jumped from my bed, arms and legs all of a tangle.

Peeping through the curtains, and past the blind,
Thoughts of magic flew through my mind.
The moon and Christmas lights shone down on the snow,
Reflecting up in the night with a bright white glow.
When with excitement my sleepy eyes opened wide,
A flying sleigh, pulled by reindeer, dashing to hide!

I turned away, my breath gave a pause,
I was sure that I'd just caught a glimpse of Santa Claus!
Even faster than rockets his reindeer came,
He held tight the harness and called each by name.
They jostled, and jangled led by a red nose,
Rudolph pushed on the reindeer as the sleigh rose.

Silently swooping across trees and roofs they fly,
His reindeers jerked and bolted through the sky.
Gone in an instant, but then I heard proof,
My ears pricked up hearing reindeer paws on the roof.
Before my eyes in a twinkling light,
Santa disappeared into the house – I knew I was right!

He wore shiny black boots and a suit all in red,
Just as the books had said that I'd read.
White fur finished his bright red coat,
The name of 'Santa' on gift labels he'd wrote.
A pack full of toys he'd brought for us all,
All shapes and sizes, and one quite tall!

His eyes had a sparkle, his cheeks were all pink,
He went to his work with no need to think.
His mouth wore a smile, his beard was bright white,
His rounded belly sat over a belt wrapped tight.
He was a little bit plump and with a big round tummy,
Tucking into a mince pie which looked rather yummy!
Placing presents at a carefully decorated tree,
I hoped I'd been good enough to have one for me.

In an instant the twinkling light was back,
Taking carrots for reindeer, he picked up his sack.

He looked up to the sky, a finger placed at his nose,
A cheeky little wink and to the roof tops he rose.

A nod to his reindeer and a quick harness thrash,
Into the night sky they flew like a flash.
With a Yo Ho Ho Ho off to spread Christmas cheer,
Santa, the reindeer and sleigh disappear.

Snowflakes continued to fall all around,
But I was sure I heard a distant sound.
Yes, there it was, I heard him loud and clear,
Merry Christmas to all and a Happy New Year!

Printed in the United States
by Baker & Taylor Publisher Services